Moochie the Soochie

Visits the Peace People

Moochie the Soochie

Visits the Peace People

by Quinton Douglas Crawford

ReadersMagnet, LLC

Moochie the Soochie: Visits the Peace People

Published in the United States of America
ISBN Paperback: 978-1-953616-88-3
ISBN Hardback: 978-1-954371-26-2
ISBN eBook: 978-1-953616-89-0

ReadersMagnet, LLC
10620 Treena Street, Suite 230 | San Diego, California, 92131 USA
1.619.354.2643 | www.readersmagnet.com

Cover design by Ericka Obando
Interior design by Shemaryl Tampus

MOOCHIE THE SOOCHIE

Fourteen days to meet the People

(Learn the Languages)

Author - Mr. Quinton Douglass Crawford (USA)

Contributing Writer - Mr. Kye Wayne Shi (of China)

Contributing Illustrator - Mr. Asad Farook (of Sri Lanka)

I am - Adebayo

On her first day Moochie came to Nigeria, a place in West Africa to find the Yoruba people. She found a friend to talk to, greeted, and said goodbye to him. In the Yoruba language Moochie said:

Bawo-Ni: which means Hello		**Or'e: which means Friend**
O'seun: which means Thank You	**and**	**O'Dabo: which means Goodbye**

We are: Arila -and- Kelia

The second day, Moochie came to Yemen and Iran, a place in Asia were the people speak Arabic. She found friends to talk to, talked and later said goodbye before leaving. In the Arabic language, she said:

Marhaba: which means Hello **Sadeek: which means Friend**

Shakura: which means Thank You **and** **Ma'a Salaama: which means Goodbye**

I am Brinda

On the third day, Moochie came to a place called Northern America, an ancient continent of natives. The people she met were the Cherokee. She found many friends to talk to, enjoyed, and said goodbye to them. In the Cherokee language, this is what she said:

Si-Yo: which means Hello **O-Gi-Na-Li: which means Friend**

Wa-Do: which means Thank You **and** **Dodadagohvi: which means Goodbye**

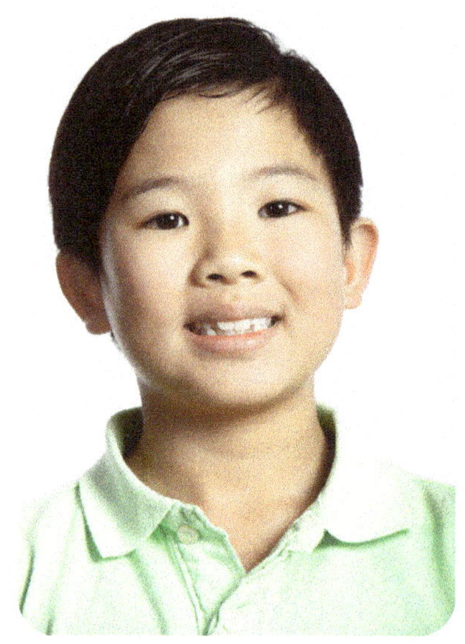

We are – Yao and Jenni

On the fourth day, Moochie came to a place called China, near an ancient place with a yellow river. She found a friend to enjoy and talk too. At the end of the day she said goodbye to them. In Mandarin, this is what Moochie said:

Ni Hao: which means Hello

Xia-Xia (Sheya Sheya sound): which means Thank You and

Ping Yao: which means Friend

Zia Jian(Zeeya Jeea-an): which means Goodbye

I am Areceli

On the fifth day, Moochie came to a place called Michoacan, in a land now called Mexico. She found friends to talk to and enjoy. She said goodbye to them, as a nice person should. In the Nahuatl language, this is what she said:

Jao: which means Hello **Niknui: which means Friend**

Tlaosojkamari: which means Thank You and **Ane': which means Goodbye**

I am - Natsuko

On the sixth day, Moochie came to a place called Japan. The people spoke very fast, with long words sounding the same. She found a friend that she wanted to talk to, greeted, enjoyed and then said goodbye to her. In the Japanese, language this is what she said:

Konnichiwa: which means Hello **Otomodachi: which means Friend**

Arigato: which means Thank You **and** **Sayonara: which means Goodbye**

I am Akela

On her seventh day, Moochie came to a place called Oahu, in a place called Hawaii. She found another friend to talk to, greeted, enjoyed, and then said goodbye to her. In the Hawaiian language, this is what she said:

Aloha: which means which means Hello **Makamaka: Friend**

Mahalo-Ole: which means Thank You **and** **Aloha: which means Goodbye**

We are Ramneek and Danika

On the eight day, Moochie came to a place called India to meet the Hindi people. She found friends that she wanted to talk to, greeted, enjoyed, and said goodbye to. In the Hindi language, she said:

Abhivadan: which means Hello **Mitta: which means Friend**

Shukriyu: which means Thank You and **Rama Rama: which means Goodbye**

I am Shanti

On her ninth day Moochie came to a place called Ghana, in a place called Kumasi among the Ashanti. She found another friend to talk to, greeted, enjoyed, and then said goodbye to her. In the Twi language she said:

Mah-yo: which means Hello

Adamfo: which means Friend

Medani: which means Thank You and

Bye-Bye: which means Goodbye

We are – Nandi and Shaka

On the tenth day Moochie came to a place called Kwa-Bulawayo, to meet the Zulu people. This language was one of her favorites to hear and speak. She found friends to talk to, greeted, enjoyed and then said goodbye to them. In the Zulu language she said:

Sawubona: which means Hello **Umn-Gahni: which means Friend**

Ngiyabonga: which means Thank You and HambaKahle:whichmeansGoodbye

I am - Patrick

On the eleventh day Moochie came to a place called Switzerland, to meet the Dutch people. She found friends to talk to, greeted, enjoyed and then said goodbye to them. In the Dutch language she said:

Hallo: which means Hello

Vriend: which means Friend

Dank-u: which means Thank You **and**

Vaarwel: which means Goodbye

I am - Hai

On the twelfth and last day, Moochie came to a place called Vietnam to meet the Vietnamese people. She found friends that she wanted to talk to, greeted, enjoyed, and said goodbye to her. This is what she said:

Hello: which means Hello

Com-on-ban: which means Thank You

Nguoi-ban: which means Friend

Tam: which means Goodbye

I am - Kiyu

On the thirteenth day Moochie came to a place called South America, to a place in Peru. She found a friend that she wanted to talk to, greeted, enjoyed herself, and then said goodbye to her as a nice person should. In the Quechua language this is what she said:

Napaykuy: which means Hello **Amigu: which means Friend**

Agradisiyki: which means Thank You **and** **Kacharpari: which means Goodbye**

I am - Dagul

On the fourteenth day Moochie came to a place currently called the Philippines.

The people spoke a language called Cebuano (Seybuano). She found a friend that she wanted to talk to, greeted, enjoyed herself, and then said goodbye to him. In the Cebuano language, this is what she said:

Kumusta: which means How Are You? **Kaibigan: which means Friend**

Salamat: which means Thank You **and** **Paalam: which means Goodbye**

MOOCHIE
THE SOOCHIE

Visits the Peace People

An International Children's Book Story- #2

Author and Illustrator: Mr. Quinton Douglass Crawford

Moochie was a time traveler that loved to share her music with peaceful people from other worlds. She looked like a purple girl, and spoke thousands of languages. She could even move herself into the past, or present with angelic sounds of a song, and a thought. She could read every language, sing many songs, but hated war and words of hate.

One day she decided to find people that loved peace as much as her by traveling through time. Moochie first traveled 5,000 years into the past from today. She decided to visit a corner of Africa, to see the smart people at the tips of the longest river.

When she arrived, she met a leader named Queen Tiye, then later met a Professor named Im-Hotep that was working on an invention called medicine. Moochie was told the name of the place she was in is called "Kemet". I would like to teach you, but I have students called Greeks in my college today.

They call our home Egypt and Nubia is to the west.

In time, jealousy and violence ruled over the visitor of (Egypt) Kemet. The visitors started to make lies, and wars, so Moochie left.

She said “I only seek places of Peace not war”, so I will choose to stay away for a few thousand years more. I shall return with you and your friends the Nubians, Ethiopians, Masai, and Moor. I shall return soon because war is a bore.

Moochie decided to travel to another place to see other peoples, read their books, and hear their words. She knew the time as 1481, and that she was in a place that was to be called Aztlan (now Mexico).

She came across a man named the great “Moctezuma II,” a leader of great power and mind. We are a people that started calling our land Aztlan. We are known as the Anahuac people, a native name of our lands, meaning "Land of Earth's People."

Our people live thousands of miles northeast, as a people called the Mississippi; in another place further northwest some are called the "Mojave," to the south of me here are our family the Guatemala. We worship life and creation.

She saw many wonders from north to south, but soon came a war, to Moochie that was a bore. From the west and the east a strange new people came. A horrible culture of pain, fighting, and theft led the invading people's desires.

Moochie decided to leave for now, and return much later when peace will begin once more. Moochie went on to another place to find many others in the past. She found a place with people named "Ch'ing". So she asked; what is the name of the place she is in?

A leader named “Qin Shi Huang” said I will tell you what land this is. We call this land China, a “Land of jewels, rivers and hidden mountains.” Here we have great ancient friends in places far away. We call them India, Tibet, and Japan, here in a year some know as 223.

The only times when peace and freedom lasted longest in places, were when women were also respected leaders. Soon wars began growing from invaders near and far, from seas, and borders with religions falsely shown. Moochie decided that it was time to leave. She promised to come back in future days to see what will develop for peaceful ways. Soon Moochie decided to go further back in time, to find a new place with no war or fights on anyone’s mind.

She found the oldest people, in a new distant place. It was not just the people called Buddhists in temples, or the people of deserts with huts shaped like circles, not the Hopi, Ashanti, or the just Aborigine dreamers, or the people in cold with bricks made of snow, but all were symbols of peace people that she searched for. The oldest civilized people living with nature, not against, were the people called the "San", a much shorter people than her. They were the oldest people anyone had found, still in existence, but displaced. Peace was so much fun here and civilized behavior was insistent.

She had to see a friend of these people only steps away. They were told to live at the beginning of the rivers Nile & Zambezi, with the largest waterfall on Earth that they call "Mosi-oa-Tunya" (The smoke that Thunders forever). What some visitors call the waters of Victoria.

When invaders came rushing bringing pains and sore division, she decided to tell the people she will return when war is no more again.

Moochie went to a new place in time and met a woman called "Envera" with a man named "Bardyllis." Envera asked her to stop for a moment, I have something to tell you. Our land is called ILLYRIA a place of our dreams; we have been friends with the Nubians of the southern lands of becoming a desert. It was 345b.c, and Moochie wanted to stay.

She considered a few thousand years more, but wars kept coming their way. So it was nearing time to go away. No peace here no more for near a 1,000 years to say.

Soon the land was divided in several new places, Moochie stood on what is called Bosnia, a land with castles, masons, and a few crazies, all founded by Moors. Moochie decided it's time to go away, to find another place were peace is obeyed. Were people made the world around them peaceful, not desolate, restless, poor, or sore. Moochie heard a name of a woman called "Zenobia" a third-century queen. She stood for justice and harmony, and peace lover with dreams. She came from Palmyra, a place in now Europe. She was a woman told of in few stories to be a peacekeeper for stories.

Odd battles came from wars in lands, and pirates of small seas. Moochie met with praying women here that were moving to the mountains, for reasons like these.

Some misguided in faiths called them evil and building them to be distrusted. Many women were forced to be servants of bad men and social disorder. Moochie went to a place meant to create agreements and order, finding good and bad people working for good with growing powers.

She soon decided to take a look into the future of people.

As she travelled into the future of now, changes were never certain. Versions of the future changed from moment to moment with every former action leading to a mix of world orders. She left to a future with many dangerous things.

Many people were in anger, frustration, and need. Moochie also looked at a future full of joy, balance and prosperity. A world of people rid of hunger, poverty, wars, and with nature. A union of people's governed justice to the world. This world she saw in decades to come; had new forests, clean oceans, and other lands looking as they should.

She went further into the future to a time unknown, to find a great time of joy, where bad people lived and flourished no more. “This seems like a great society,” she said with glee. So she landed in a time of peace, no war, or poverty in any place anymore. All cultures existed with ways ancient and modern; the biggest change was that money was not to be bothered.

United Earth Government
(Circa 2154)

They knew all world history, mathematics, sciences, languages, music, and sports. They enhanced useful ancient practices with the new technologies of the time, and formed better societies with honor and no blight. They supported themselves with nature much more.

The end times of trauma, and no hope were over and all good people took over. The people and leaders of the days after then; had realized the ignorance of people before them. Crime and rudeness was soon a hard to find, because there was no reason to be that way again.

They worked hard and well to restore the skies, oceans, rivers, forests and other placed they harmed. The people finally realized they cannot live without a healthy world of life to live on. Before Moochie went back to home, she had to go to the party, as she promised to do for her friend named Khamila, a princess of Zimbabwe.

Moochie tapped a beat, sung a song and appeared on an island, were the people danced to the waves, and moved like the waters. It sounded like her mother's voice, as they swayed like the ocean and she wondered what is the name of this magical motion? Here in the year 1840 she asked "Queen Liliuokalani," why they were doing this incredible dance slow and in sudden hurries.

Moochie asked her what place am I in with so much fun. The queen said our lands are called "Hawaii," and you may stay here for your time. Soon a group of people came here to take over their lands, with war and destruction symbols on head. It was time to go back to finish a journey, to return to the places were peace filled it's promise.

The Queen said our dance is of the spirit for life, balance, and powers; it is called the HULA my friend, please join us for awhile. Her people use dance to tell many stories, and this was also true from some people called humans. With fun on her mind, and joy in her motions, Moochie told stories of past and songs of good fortune. When the party was over she went back to her home, and promised to return again when world peace was a norm.

To be continued...

Essential Facts for the change of today for tomorrow

Most of the human population is female.

It is the job of every generation to prepare a better environment for the next generation, because radical change can occur within one generation.

When studying world history, continually ask the questions

Who were the women in leadership? (Herstory)

Who were the good men?

Who were the bad men?

What was the relationship with nature?

What are the perspectives of others, especially the natives?

Quote of the Day

To lead a life in which we are inspired and can inspire others.

Our hearts have to be alive; they have to filled with passion and enthusiasm. To achieve that, we need the courage to live true to ourselves. Rather than borrowing from or imitating others, we need the conviction to be able to think for ourselves and to take action out of our own sense of responsibility.

www.ingramcontent.com/pod-product-compliance
Ingram Content Group UK Ltd.
Pitfield, Milton Keynes, MK11 3LW, UK
UKHW062300290726
14090UKWH00017B/805